11159

1615
CROSS OF GOLD

Mary Z. Holmes
Illustrated by Geri Strigenz

STONE
BANK
BOOKS

RAINTREE
STECK-VAUGHN
L I B R A R Y
Austin, Texas

For Jo

This text and art were reviewed for accuracy by Orlando Romero, Head Research Librarian, History Library, Museum of New Mexico, Santa Fe, NM.

Designed by Geri Strigenz

Published by Raintree/Steck-Vaughn Library
P.O. Box 26015, Austin Tx 78755

Library of Congress Cataloging-in-Publication Data
Holmes, Mary Z.
    Cross of gold / Mary Z. Holmes ; illustrated by Geri Strigenz.
       p. cm. — (History's children)
    "A Stone Bank Book"
    Summary: In 1615, a friar sent to Santa Fe by the Viceroy of New Spain meets a boy who shares his concern for the local Indians and who helps him determine the future of this small outpost town.
    ISBN 0-8114-3507-5. — ISBN 0-8114-6432-6 (pbk.)
    1. New Mexico—History—To 1848—Juvenile fiction. [1. New Mexico—History—to1848—Fiction. 2. Spaniards—New Mexico—Fiction.] I. Strigenz, Geri K., ill. II. Title. III. Series: Holmes, Mary Z. History's children.
PZ7.H7375Cr 1992   91-37280
[Fic]—dc20   CIP AC

Printed in the United States of America
1 2 3 4 5 6 7 8 9 WZ 96 95 94 93 92

1615

*T*his story takes place in the small outpost town of Santa Fe, in what is now the state of New Mexico. In 1615, only a small number of Spanish settlers and missionaries live here. They rule over the many Indians in the area.

The Spanish are a long way from Mexico City, the capital of their empire in the Americas. Few visitors or supplies ever reach them. They don't have much furniture, and clothes must last for many years. Their houses are adobe, made of mud bricks with dirt floors.

LIST OF CHARACTERS

Felipe de Ávila	(feh-LEE-peh day AH-vee-lah)
Felipe's father, Vicente	(vee-CEN-teh)
Felipe's mother, Eufemia	(u-FAY-mee-ah)
Felipe's brother, Alonso	(ah-LOAN-so)
Alonso's wife, Catalina	(kat-ah-LEE-nah)
Alonso's son, Marcos	(MAR-kos)
Damiana de Rosas	(dah-mee-AH-nah day RO-sas)
Friar Nicolás Ayeta	(nee-ko-LAS ah-YEH-tah)
Friar Pedro	(PEH-dro)
Friar Martín	(mar-TEEN)

HISTORICAL PERSONAGES

Governor Ceballos	(say-BAH-yos)
Custodio Ordóñez	(koos-TOE-dee-o or-DOAN-yez)

PLACES

Santa Fe	(san-tah FEH)
Nambe	(nam-BEH)
San Ildefonso	(san ill-deh-FOAN-so)
Taos	(TAH-ous)
Acoma	(AH-ko-mah)

I

FELIPE DE ÁVILA

Friar Nicolás's diary:

I am Friar Nicolás Ayeta. I am writing from the kingdom of New Mexico in the year of our Lord 1615.

His Excellency the Viceroy sent me here from Mexico in the south. He wants me to inform him about this troubled land.

I am a Franciscan friar — a priest of the Holy Order of St. Francis. Now I am also a spy.

I came a long way from Mexico City to reach the Kingdom of New Mexico. The journey took six months. That should have been time enough to figure out why His Excellency chose me to do this job. But even after all this time, I still do not know why he did it. The Viceroy must have many other men who are better spies than I am.

The church asked me to do this for the Viceroy. I was told not to let anyone know why I came to New Mexico, not even my brother friars. How could I refuse these holy orders?

I arrived at Santa Fe in June. I met all the Spaniards there, though there are very few of them. Only about one hundred and fifty people live in Santa Fe. A dozen or so friars live at the missions in this kingdom. They all believe I am here to study the life of the New Mexican Indians. They are wrong, because I am here to spy on them.

I haven't written to the Viceroy yet. I am not sure what I should say to him.

At present, I am taking care of a boy who is very ill. Perhaps he is dying. We are at the Indian town of Taos, waiting to see what happens. When the boy wakes up from his fevered sleep, he begs me to write his story. It seems to mean a great deal to him. So I have promised to write each word faithfully.

The boy's name is Felipe de Ávila. He is named after King Felipe III of Spain, so he tells me. His age is fourteen. This is his story.

* * *

Felipe's story:

The festival day in June began with morning Mass. We knelt on the dirt floor of our Santa Fe church to bless the feast day of St. John the Baptist. I prayed for help in serving God our Lord and Spain with honor.

Marcos poked me. "Pray to find gold, Felipe."

I gave him a dark look. Marcos was my nephew. As his uncle, I deserved more respect than he gave me. But, because he was two weeks older, he felt he could tell me what to do.

"I already did," I whispered. I asked every time I prayed. Marcos and I dreamed of gaining great honor and wealth by discovering gold in New Mexico. It was the dream of many men who came to this new Spanish kingdom.

At the end of Mass, we waited as Governor Ceballos rose from his chair. He led us from the church.

The women were dressed in their finest festival clothes. Damiana de Rosas wore a red velvet gown that set off her dark hair. As she stepped from the church into the sunlight, she looked at me and smiled. Marcos pushed me aside and bowed to her. Damiana laughed and hurried after her family.

I grabbed Marcos by the arm. "She thinks you're a fool."

"She thinks I'm wonderful," Marcos said. "She'll love me when she sees me in the military show." He swung an imaginary sword at me. We ran across the plaza to the soldiers' corral.

Today's festival would be very different from those in the past. It wouldn't be as grand as last year, when we had more people in Santa Fe. Since then, many of them had returned to Mexico. There were few of us left now. Even the number of soldiers remaining in Santa Fe was small. That's why my brother, Captain Alonso de Ávila, asked that Marcos and I ride in the military show today.

Marcos and I were not old enough to be soldiers. However,we were well trained in fighting and horsemanship. I couldn't remember a time when I didn't know how to ride. Marcos thought he was the better rider. I didn't agree. Marcos was good, but I was excellent.

My father, Vicente de Ávila, was putting on his armor. An Indian servant helped him with the steel helmet, breastplate, and shoulder, arm, and leg pieces. My father was a clerk in the Governor's office, not a soldier. But he had his own armor, as every gentleman did. And when needed, he fought with the soldiers to defend us against hostile Indians. When I grew up and became a soldier, he would give this armor to me.

My father stood straight and tall. He was becoming an old man, but I thought he was still good-looking with his trimmed white beard, proud posture, and fine armor.

"Felipe, wear this coat of chain mail," Father said as I hurried to him. "You'll ride next to me."

"Thank you, Father," I said. The servant helped me slip the coat of mail over my head and handed me a helmet. I strapped on the belt and sword my father had given me. Then I took a lance and shield. I already had on my best linen shirt, breeches, and fine leather boots. Damiana would be very impressed.

"That will do very well," Father said as he fixed my helmet. "You look like Alonso when he was your age." He looked at me fondly. I was his second son, born after my brother was grown and had a son of his own. "Make me proud of you today, Felipe," he said.

"Don't worry, Father," I said with a smile. I hurried across the corral to find my horse.

As we mounted our horses and lined up with the soldiers, I saw that Marcos also wore a coat of mail. He winked at me as the call sounded.

"March!" The order to begin was given.

We rode out into the plaza with banners flying. Trumpet and drum sounded, and guns boomed. The sun lighted the steel of armor and shields. Some of these men were of the group that had won and settled New Mexico for the Spanish king seventeen years ago. Both my father and brother had taken part. I was proud to ride with these *conquistadors* [conquerors].

The feet of our horses stirred the dust on the ground as we rode in a clean line. We passed by the cheering Governor, women, friars, and Indians. I sat straight in the saddle and held my head high. What a shame there were so few people to watch us.

The soldiers divided into two groups and went to either end of the plaza. Then we rushed at each other, as if it were a real battle charge. Meeting in the middle, we pretended to fight. Lances crashed into shields, horses cried, and the dust rose.

I took a blow to my arm, but the soldier was careful not to use enough power to knock me off my horse. Another soldier shot directly at me with a loud bang. I was thankful he wasn't using bullets. The battle went on. It was noisy and a little frightening. In short, it was splendid.

When the battle ended, we were free to leave. Some of the soldiers stayed to display their horsemanship. Marcos and I put our horses through their paces to show how good we were too.

"We'll be soldiers soon," I shouted to Marcos.

"Not soon enough for me," he called back. He rode to my side, and we galloped around the plaza.

"And rich," I laughed, "if we find gold." I looked to see if Damiana was watching us. She wasn't.

Marcos said, "*When* we find gold, Felipe. Not *if.*"

I left his side to ride alone. I saw that Father and Alonso had dismounted and already removed their armor. They were talking to Governor Ceballos, who pointed at me and then at Marcos. I hoped he was saying good things about both of us.

I saw my mother, Eufemia de Ávila. And there was Alonso's wife, Catalina, with the other women. I rode over to them and dismounted.

"Well done, *conquistador*," my mother said. "All the ladies saw how well you rode."

Damiana de Rosas heard her. She turned to me and said, "Yes, Felipe, the ladies are proud of you."

"Even the young ladies?" I asked. She blushed and nodded.

As I walked my horse to cool it down, Damiana followed at my side. She's a beautiful girl, I thought. I didn't know what to say to her.

"I enjoyed the mock battle, Felipe," she said. "It seemed so real. I was frightened for you."

Someone tapped my shoulder. I turned sharply, thinking it must be Marcos. He always appeared when I talked to Damiana. But it wasn't Marcos. It was a tall, thin friar with amazingly black eyes. A stranger. I gasped in surprise.

"I am Friar Nicolás Ayeta," he said. "I just arrived in Santa Fe. I have not had the pleasure of meeting you."

As I stared into his dark eyes, I felt that something extraordinary was about to happen in my life.

* * *

Friar Nicolás's diary:

The fever has taken Felipe again, and he is asleep. What a terrible sickness.

I remember how startled he was when I introduced myself that day. I gave it no special meaning at the time. Now I have come to wonder. Did Felipe somehow know that the two of us would play a part in the events to come?

II

TRIBUTE COLLECTION

Friar Nicolás's diary:
When I was ordered to come here, I didn't know what I would find. This place is not like Mexico with its big Spanish cities and peaceful Indians.

Only a handful of Spaniards are here. Their town, Santa Fe, is a poor, little place hundreds of miles from anything. Holy faith. That's what Santa Fe means. Indeed, they need faith to live among the tens of thousands of Indians in this vast wilderness.

Here, the Indians are the ones who have large towns, or pueblos, as they are called. By my count, there are more than thirty pueblos. Some of the huge adobe pueblos are up to seven stories tall. Hundreds of Indians live in them.

Who are these Spanish people who stay in Santa Fe under such conditions? And why do they stay?

Felipe talks about finding gold. Bah! After all, the Spanish settled here seventeen years ago. They explored the territory widely. No one found silver or gold — or anything of value, if the truth be known. None of them, except for boys like Felipe and Marcos, dream of gold anymore.

Felipe is waking up. He looks around weakly and asks if I have my pen and paper ready. I give him water to drink and offer food, but he refuses. He wants to go on with his story.

* * *

Felipe's story:

For several days after the festival, Marcos and I busied ourselves in the usual way. We spent many hours riding and practicing with our swords. We checked on the Indian servants who minded our crops and watched our cattle, sheep, and goats grazing in the foothills. In the heat of the day, we lay under cottonwood trees along the creek and made plans to find gold.

One night, Marcos and I sat with a soldier at the bonfire burning in the plaza. We were listening to his adventures. Alonso came to remind us of the hour and bring us home where we all lived together — my parents, Alonso, his wife, Marcos, and me.

As we walked to the house, Alonso said, "I'm taking soldiers up to Nambe pueblo to collect tribute from the Indians. The two of you may come along if you wish. You'll have only a few hours to sleep before we leave."

"We do wish!" Marcos and I said eagerly.

Each year, every Indian family gave a woven blanket and a few baskets of corn as tribute. Then these were divided among our families in Santa Fe. Perhaps *gave* is not the right word. In truth, since we had conquered them, we *took* what we needed. Still, it was an honor to be asked to go along.

I was excited and couldn't sleep. It wasn't long before Alonso told us to get up. The night air was cold, so we slipped into our jackets before going out. The plaza was already busy. Oxen, tied to two-wheeled carts, blew steam from their noses. The horses danced in the light of the bonfire, pulling against their ropes.

"This will be a slow trip," Alonso said as he mounted, "so take it easy. Ride behind the carts and see that the Indians keep them moving."

With a full moon lighting the night, the soldiers led the way from the plaza. The stranger, Friar Nicolás, joined the group. The carts followed, guided by Indian servants who walked next to them. Marcos and I rode behind.

13

I saw Damiana at the door of her house with a blanket thrown over her shoulders. I saluted her. She waved back, calling, "God keep you both safe."

We headed north out of town. First, we passed through the fields of wheat, oats, and barley behind the government buildings. Ahead, over the low foothills, lay the way to Nambe pueblo. I looked at Marcos. Even though I couldn't see his face clearly in the dark, I knew he was smiling.

The train of carts made its way slowly through the night. Finally, the sun rose over the mountains in the east. The snow on the mountaintops had melted only a few weeks ago. Now they were shaded in early morning shadow and covered with a violet haze. When lit by the western sun at sunset, the mountains would look as red as blood.

The twenty-mile journey took us many hours. Twice I shouted to Marcos, who fell asleep as he watched the slow bobbing heads of the oxen. The soldiers sang and told wild, funny stories. Alonso called back to us. "Don't believe everything they say."

Around noon, the oxen pulling the last cart turned away from the train. The Indians couldn't turn them back. One of the soldiers came galloping to the cart. He used his whip to make the oxen get back in line.

Then his whip lashed out at the Indians who had let this happen. They fell to the ground before his horse. He struck them again and again until his anger passed. I felt sick to my stomach and turned away. It was too ugly to watch.

Alonso came riding from the front of the train. Grabbing the whip from the soldier, he ordered him to stop.

"Put the Indians in a cart at the front," Alonso said to the soldier. "They'll ride the rest of the way."

Friar Nicholás seemed about to speak, but kept silent.

After that, Marcos and I rode on each side of the cart. The stubborn oxen wanted to go their own way. We poked at them with sticks to keep them going straight. Once they stopped and refused to move. I dismounted to start the oxen moving again and walked next to them for a time.

15

"You don't look like a *conquistador* now," Marcos laughed.

I didn't think it was funny. I frowned at him and said, "And you didn't look like a *conquistador* when you fell asleep on your horse." I wasn't really angry at Marcos. I felt sick about the whipping.

Marcos hung his head and said, "I'm sorry, Your Excellency Uncle Felipe." I smiled. Marcos could always make me feel better. Although we enjoyed ourselves those last hours before reaching Nambe, I kept thinking about the whipped Indians. Maybe when I was grown, I could stop such things.

When we arrived at the pueblo in early evening, the bell at the small church rang to welcome us. The Tewa Indians climbed down the ladders of their homes to see what was happening. Others came running in from their corn fields. When they saw the empty carts that meant we had come for blankets and corn, they glared at the soldiers. They must hate us, I thought.

Friar Pedro invited us to evening Mass at his adobe church. "Then eat with us," he said. "There is time to collect tribute in the morning."

Having time to explore Nambe before Mass, I scrambled up a ladder of the pueblo with Marcos following. We stood there on the roof, looking out over the land. We could see for many miles. The setting sun made the earth turn deep red. The mountains to the east changed color before our eyes.

"We must make a plan to get to the Taos pueblo," I said to Marcos. "From there we can go into the mountains."

"To search for gold?" he asked.

I nodded. "Yes. I've got a feeling about that place." Seven-story Taos lay many more miles to the northeast. There the mountains rose sharply behind the Indian town. That's where I want to go, I thought, as we returned to our group below.

Friar Pedro led Mass. The Tewas sang and chanted prayers the friar had taught them. Later, they served us food grown in their fields. Marcos and I lay down outside near a bonfire, wrapped in blankets to keep warm in the chilly summer night. I saw Friar Nicolás sitting alone, staring into the fire. The low, mumbling talk of the soldiers was putting me to sleep. The Tewas were quiet. They were sleeping too.

As each Tewa family came forward the next morning, it delivered a blanket and baskets of corn. Our servants loaded the goods in the carts. Alonso and Friar Pedro kept track of each offering. Then, the last family gave only corn.

"Tell them to give a blanket as everyone else is doing," Alonso instructed the friar, who could speak the Tewa language.

Friar Pedro spoke to the family, but the Tewa father shook his head. "He has no blanket for you," said the friar.

"Then I will take what he is wearing," Alonso said, as a soldier stepped forward to take the woven blanket from the Tewa.

Friar Pedro said that this Indian would have nothing to keep him warm. It was his only blanket. I closed my eyes. Please, Alonso, I thought, please don't do it.

Alonso stood silently. Finally, he told the soldier to forget the blanket. He ordered us to get on our horses.

"Governor Ceballos thanks you for the gifts. You have pleased him very much." Alonso asked the friar to translate this for the Tewas. Then he gave us the order to leave Nambe.

As the train of filled carts slowly made its way home to Santa Fe, I thought about what I'd seen. And I began to have an uneasy feeling about Friar Nicolás. He didn't talk at all on the way home. I felt he was watching us very closely.

* * *

Friar Nicolás's diary:

I was. I remember that day very well.

Felipe's eyes are glassy and full of fever. He pauses often as he remembers these events. Sometimes, I think he is sleeping once more, but then he goes on with the story. I don't believe he remembers who I am.

17

III

FRIAR NICOLÁS

Felipe's story:

"Eufemia," my father said.

Mother looked up from her mending. "Yes, Vicente."

"This Friar Nicolás has been to see me in the government offices," he said, turning from the window to face her.

"What does he want?" Mother's questions always went to the heart of matters. I listened closely to my father's reply.

Father frowned. "He doesn't really say. That's what worries me. We have pleasant talks about nothing. Then he slips in questions about last year's trouble. I try not to answer."

"What does Governor Ceballos say?" Mother asked.

Father shrugged, meaning that Governor Ceballos didn't know what Friar Nicolás wanted either. "Even the other friars are worried when he's around. I don't believe they trust him."

"Does he work for Custodio Ordóñez?" she asked.

The Custodio was the head of the friars in New Mexico. He was the one who had caused us so much trouble. He put our last governor in prison. And he said he would throw many of us out of the church. Finally, when Governor Ceballos came here, the old governor was sent to Mexico City for questioning. Many of the frightened settlers went back too. My family decided to stay. But we were still afraid of the Custodio. No one wanted to be thrown out of the church. Our faith was very important to us. As important as food.

"Custodio Ordóñez stays at the Santo Domingo pueblo," Father answered. "He hasn't caused trouble since Friar Nicolás came. The opinion of the other friars is that the Custodio is worried too."

A servant came into the room with cups of hot chocolate for us to drink.

Father took a sip and said, "No one knows why Friar Nicolás is here or who sent him. And now, he's asked for someone to take him to Taos pueblo." He put his cup on the windowsill.

Taos, I thought.

Father went on. "Of course, soldiers must go to keep him safe. But Governor Ceballos can't think who to send with Friar Nicolás as a companion. It must be someone who can't reveal anything that could hurt us."

"I have an idea, Father," I blurted out. "Send Marcos and me."

That's how Marcos and I ended up in the Governor's office. We explained how we could go with Friar Nicolás to Taos. Sending boys instead of a government official like my father sounded good to him. We were told not to say anything that could hurt our people.

"Like what?" asked Marcos.

"That's what we don't know," Governor Ceballos said, shaking his head. "You had best keep everything to yourselves. Pretend you don't know anything, boys."

That won't be hard for Marcos, I thought.

In a few days, everything was ready for the trip. Friar Nicolás wanted to spend several days at Taos. During this time, Marcos and I planned to sneak off into the mountains to search for gold. Trying not to let Marcos see, I slipped off to say good-by to Damiana. Marcos had already talked to her, she told me. That didn't make me very happy.

During the first part of the trip, no one talked at all. The soldiers rode on ahead while Marcos and I stayed close to Friar Nicolás. I was glad he didn't ask any questions. We stopped that afternoon at San Ildefonso pueblo, located near the Rio del Norte [River of the North, now called the Rio Grande].

A crowd of Tewas stood around Friar Martín, who ran the mission church at San Ildefonso. The hair of three Tewa men had been cut, and they hung their heads in shame. Friar Martín was whipping a fourth Indian. These Indians were now Christians. Friar Martín had caught them doing an old Tewa dance in a *kiva* [an underground Tewa ceremony room]. This was forbidden by the church. Today he was punishing them. Not more whipping, I thought. I didn't want to watch.

The crowd parted as Friar Nicolás rode his mule through. "Friar Martín," he said with a heavy frown over his dark eyes. "Do you not welcome a fellow Franciscan?"

Friar Martín dropped the whip. "Who are you?" he asked. The whipped Tewa crawled away and disappeared into the crowd.

"I am Friar Nicolás Ayeta of Mexico City. I have come to spend the night at San Ildefonso," he said.

From the look on Friar Martín's face, I could see that he knew of Friar Nicolás and wasn't pleased to see him. I glanced at Marcos to see if he noticed this, but Marcos wasn't paying attention. Some Tewa boys were waving to him to come. Marcos started toward them. I followed.

"They want to have a foot race with us," Marcos said as the boys made signs to show running. "Shall we?"

After the long ride, I was ready for some action, and I agreed. We took off our boots and unlaced our sleeves. Marcos jumped up and down to loosen his legs. A Tewa boy pointed to the black mesa, the steep hill in the distance. We would run to the mesa and back, a long run. I wasn't so sure I could make it, but I would try for the glory of Spain.

With a great yelling and whooping, we began the run. Marcos pulled out in front and pushed hard. He's crazy, I thought. He'll never keep it up. Soon a Tewa was running next to him, matching his pace with that of Marcos. Another Tewa ran next to me.

The race took forever, and I was getting out of breath. Although I expected Marcos to fall over any minute, he didn't. He and the Tewa pushed on stride for stride, getting farther ahead of me. As we neared the pueblo again, it was certain that the two of them would win. Then, without warning, Marcos crashed into an Indian who crossed his path. They both tumbled to the ground.

I fell to the ground next to Marcos, laughing and breathless. "A valiant ending, Marcos," I said. He rolled over and moaned.

Friar Nicolás walked over. Maybe he thinks Marcos is hurt, I thought. Instead of helping Marcos, Friar Nicolás reached down to help the Indian stand, and handed him his crutch. The man had only one foot. I knew what that meant.

Marcos pointed at the Indian and said, "Acoma!"

"Acoma?" Friar Nicolás asked.

"This man was in the battle at Acoma, the sky city," Marcos said as he got up. "Don't you know about Acoma?"

"Perhaps you could tell me," invited Friar Nicolás. He sat under a cottonwood tree and patted the ground next to him. Marcos joined him.

No, I thought. Once Marcos got started on Acoma, he wouldn't stop. We were told not to tell the friar anything. Worried, I sat on the ground near them, ready to stop Marcos if I had to.

Marcos began. "It was the first winter that the settlers were in New Mexico, in 1598. Do you know Vicente de Ávila? My grandfather and Felipe's father. He came here then. Do you know Alonso de Ávila? My father and Felipe's brother, a great soldier. He was here then." Marcos talked so fast, Friar Nicolás didn't have time to say if he knew our family or not.

"What was I going to say next?" Marcos asked.

"Acoma?" Friar Nicolás prompted.

"Yes," Marcos said and took a great breath. "Acoma is a pueblo built like a fortress on a rock mesa nearly four hundred feet high. It's across the Rio del Norte and far southwest. Some of our soldiers went there. They climbed the cliff to meet the Indians of Acoma, and the Indians killed them. Some of the soldiers jumped from the cliffs. My father was not there that day."

Marcos continued, "Those soldiers who lived came back to tell the Governor. A few weeks later, in January of 1599, seventy

soldiers went back to Acoma. My father and grandfather were with them. They killed hundreds of Indians, took many as prisoners, and burned the city."

Marcos looked around for the Indian with one foot and pointed. "He was at Acoma. The Governor ordered the male prisoners to have one foot cut off," he finished with a smile. "This was before Felipe and I were born."

I shivered, as I did whenever I heard about this harsh action. I couldn't tell what Friar Nicolás was thinking. Just as he was about to speak, the mission bell called us to evening Mass.

After dark, Marcos and I bedded down near a fire. I saw Friar Nicolás and Friar Martín at the door of the small adobe church. Friar Martín was explaining the trouble he was having with the Tewas here at San Ildefonso. Some of them still danced the forbidden Tewa dances, and the friar had to punish them. Cutting hair and whipping were only two punishments. For the worst of the Tewas, there was another. Tomorrow he would take four of the Indians to Custodio Ordóñez at Santo Domingo. From there, the Indians would be taken to Mexico and sold as slaves.

Friar Nicolás came over to the fire. He sat alone and stared into it. "Who is the enemy here?" he said. "Who is the enemy here?"

I wondered what he was talking about. The Tewas? The Indians of Acoma? I was keeping my eye on him. He didn't know I was awake.

IV

THE MOUNTAINS

Friar Nicolás's diary:

The Viceroy wants my opinion on whether to pull out of New Mexico. He hears nothing but bad things about this place. Should he bring the settlers and friars back home?

The trouble is power. Custodio Ordóñez wants the settlers to leave New Mexico to the friars. The settlers want the Custodio to stay out of their lives. It is a question of who should have power over the other.

The friars have been told to bring the Indians to Christ. Nothing must stand in the way. The settlers have been given permission to take tribute from the Indians and use them for work. The King has said so. Who has the power to decide how the Indians are used? Perhaps this cannot work.

His Excellency is tired of it. So I am here to decide for myself and let him know. What can I say? Should the Spanish leave New Mexico? Should they stay? I do not know. I pray for a sign from my Heavenly Father to show me the way.

Felipe and Marcos would have been upset if they had known what I was thinking on that trip to Taos.

* * *

Felipe's story:

We left San Ildefonso behind the next day and followed the Rio del Norte on the way to Taos. The soldiers rode in the lead with the pack mules. Marcos and I came next. We whispered about our plans to look for gold in the mountains beyond Taos. Friar Nicolás followed behind. Again, we rode for many hours without speaking to him.

The air was brilliant and clear, and the temperature just right for riding. We rode hard and made good time along the river valley. At times, the valley widened between towering cliffs on each side of the river. In some places, the river flowed through a steep canyon, and we had to watch for falling rocks.

Toward the end of the journey, Taos pueblo was in sight across a wide valley. Then Marcos broke the silence and asked, "Where are you from, Friar Nicolás?"

"I lived in many places in Mexico, Marcos," he replied. "I was born in the Mexico City. But as a friar, I have worked in the missions from Santa Barbara in the north to those in the far south."

"With the Indians?" Marcos asked.

"Yes."

"Do they live in pueblos as our Indians do?" he asked. Marcos and I were not well educated. We knew little of other places.

Friar Nicolás shook his head. "No, they once had great stone cities, decorated with gold."

Marcos gasped. "They are rich?"

"Not anymore. When the Spanish gained power over the country, they took all the riches from the Indians. Now the Indians are poor. And there are not very many left. Many died."

"Did the *conquistadors* kill them?" asked Marcos.

"They killed some," Friar Nicolás answered. "Thousands more died from Spanish sicknesses. The silver mines killed many more. When silver was discovered, the Indians were used as slaves in the mines. Thousands died."

Friar Nicolás looked directly at me. "Spanish ways are very dangerous to the Indian," he said. His dark eyes seemed to burn a hole right through me. I don't know why, but I shuddered.

We arrived at Taos and helped Friar Nicolás unpack his things. The Tiwa Indians of Taos made us welcome.

There was no mission church at Taos, only a small adobe room used by the friars when they came to preach to the Indians. This was where Friar Nicolás would stay.

At this point I put our plan into play. I told the soldiers that my brother had ordered Marcos and me to go into the mountains. Of course, that was a lie. We would be gone for two weeks. During that time, the soldiers must stay with the friar, I told them. They believed it!

At last, our great adventure was about to begin. Friar Nicolás gave us God's blessing. To be honest, I was happy to get away from him. We rode from the pueblo and began the climb into the great mountains beyond. Looking back through the aspen and pine trees, the Tiwa town seemed small. I soon forgot about it entirely.

We climbed to the top of the first ridge. Then we headed north to the higher mountains in the distance. Both of us were singing loudly, making an awful noise. We were on top of the world.

"Exactly how are we going to do this?" Marcos asked at our first night's camp. He chewed off a piece of dried beef.

I looked up from where I was spreading out blankets. "First, we'll go farther north. Then we'll start looking for gold."

"Let's search here," he said. I saw that I'm-older-than-you look in his eyes.

"It would be a waste of time," I said. "Alonso said this area has already been explored."

"Well, they could have missed the gold," he said stubbornly.

I was getting angry. I gave him my I'm-your-uncle look. "No, Marcos. We're not going to spend any time looking for gold here. It's a stupid idea."

"Who made you king?" He turned his back on me.

That's how the first two days of our adventure went. I tried to be in charge, and Marcos disagreed with everything I decided. Once, he said he wouldn't go any farther. I just kept going. When I looked back, I saw he was following me.

At the end of the third day, we reached the place high in the mountains where I wanted to begin the search. This area hadn't been explored. We made camp at the edge of a mountain stream and ate our food. By then, Marcos wasn't even speaking to me. I expected him to cheer up by morning.

I was right. He was up at dawn rummaging through our packs. "Come on, Felipe. Get up. We've got work to do, gold to find," he said. He was off into the trees before I could sit up.

I spent the day sifting through the silt at the bottom of the stream and moving from one place along the bank to another. It was hard work. I entertained myself by making up talks with Damiana in which I was witty and she adored me. As in real life, Marcos popped into my fantasy, said something silly, and made Damiana laugh. Did she like him better than she liked me? He made her laugh. I made her blush. Who could tell with girls?

Just as I was thinking what a bother Marcos was, I saw him coming down the stream. "Find anything?" I called.

"Not yet," he yelled back. "We should look upstream. Let's move camp before it gets dark."

Not wanting to start another fight between us, I let him have his way. So we packed up and led the horses higher up the mountain. It was dark by the time we settled in.

"Tell me, Marcos," I asked that night. "How do you know if a girl is fond of you?"

He was almost asleep. "That's easy," he mumbled. "If she laughs." Then he started snoring. I wanted to punch him.

Although we worked hard for two days at the new location, we saw no sign of gold. Marcos was getting restless. In the afternoon of the second day, he stopped his search and went hunting instead. I was getting tired and feeling a little sick. I decided to move back to the earlier spot, and I had packed up our camp by the time Marcos returned.

When I told him about the move, he didn't say much. I sensed that he was making an effort to hold his anger in.

"I have a feeling about the other place, Marcos," I tried to explain. "Just give me a few more days there."

He stomped off. "It always has to be your way."

We made the move, but the peace between us didn't last. As we were working the next day, I felt I was getting a fever and stopped to take a long rest. Marcos ordered me back to work.

"This is your spot, Felipe," he said. "We came all the way back here at your command. If you're not going to work, then we're going back to Taos."

Maybe it was the fever. Or maybe I'd finally had enough of him. In any case, I lost my temper and grabbed him by the arm. He shook me off and spun around to face me.

"I'm going back," he shouted. "Are you coming with me?"

"No!"

He took a swing at me, and I ducked out of the way. "I'm leaving," he shouted again. "Are you coming?"

"No!"

Marcos took another swing at me, and it connected with my jaw. Then we were wrestling on the ground. I pinned him down and said, "I'm staying, and you're staying too." We rolled over and over until he tossed me off. I landed with a thud next to the stream. I couldn't get up.

"I'm going back," he said, standing over me. "Are you coming with me?"

A wave of dizziness came over me as I looked up at him. All I could do was shake my head. Marcos brushed the dirt off his clothes and headed toward the camp. I heard him packing up. I heard him saddle his horse. I heard him muttering about me. I heard him riding away. Then I didn't hear anything. I think I passed out.

* * *

Friar Nicolás:

Marcos did return to Taos from the mountains after only a week and left on his own for Santa Fe. He told me that Felipe would come back as planned. I remember wondering at the time if something had gone wrong between them.

31

V

THE BARGAIN

Felipe's story:

When I woke up some time later, I was lying on the ground next to the stream. I crawled forward a short way to get a drink of water. My head was pounding, and I felt shivery and sick.

Then I must have slept through the night, because it was early morning when I next opened my eyes. The light made my head hurt. I felt my head to see if there was a bump or a bruise, but didn't find anything. I'm not injured, I thought. I didn't hurt my head when I fell. Marcos didn't hurt me.

It was only then that I realized I was very sick. It was as if thinking about it made me feel worse, and I vomited on the ground. I was freezing. Pulling myself to my feet, I staggered over to get a blanket and wrapped myself in it. I sat down and leaned against a tree along the stream, feeling very much alone. Having been trained in warfare, I was not afraid to face an enemy. But sickness was an unseen enemy against which I couldn't defend myself. I was afraid.

"Divine Father in Heaven," I prayed. "Hear my prayer and make me well. Help me get home again." I said the rosary of the Blessed Virgin.

Clutching the rosary beads in my hand, I passed out again. Thirst woke me up. My throat was dry and painful. I crawled to the stream and drank. When I lifted my head from the water, I saw something just below the surface. I couldn't believe it.

A burst of energy hit me. I reached into the cold mountain stream and pulled out a nugget as big as my fist. I turned it over and over in my hands.

"Gold! Felipe de Ávila has found gold!" I shouted to the trees. I laughed and laughed. If only Marcos had been there. How he would have carried on about riches, honor, and glory.

That's when I did some serious thinking. Most important was to realize that I was dangerously ill and had to be careful. Marcos wouldn't be back to get me — when he got mad, it lasted a long time. I needed a plan for rest and riding in order to get back to Taos safely by myself. I needed to eat.

Next, this place needed to be mapped so I could find it again. I thought it would be a good idea to cut trees and arrange stones to mark my way back to Taos. That would leave a trail. But to be sure, I would draw a map on an extra linen shirt from my pack, using a burned stick from the fire.

The temptation to find more gold was very strong. In the end, I decided to spend the rest of this day searching. It wasn't a wise choice, but I couldn't resist. By sunset, I had five more nuggets, a fortune in gold!

As I lay shivering under my blankets that night, I seemed to see the face of Friar Nicolás floating above me. "Who is the enemy here?" he asked me. "Who is the enemy here?" It was the fever talking. I was restless all night.

The next day I did my best to follow my plan of riding and resting. But I couldn't eat, and I was getting weaker and weaker. As I rode down one slope and up another, on and on, I thought I saw Damiana in the plaza at Santa Fe. Another time, I thought the Indian with one foot was following me.

It was difficult to stay on my horse. I wondered how Marcos could sleep on horseback without falling off. When I dozed, I would wake with a start to find myself leaning off to one side of the saddle and have to catch myself before I slid to the ground. During a stop for rest, I worked on the map before I fell into a deep

sleep. In my dreams, Friar Nicolás was chasing me. I ran, and he shouted after me, "Thousands died, Felipe." I ran faster with my hands over my ears, but he called louder and louder. "Get away," I cried. Then I woke up. It was night, and I was very cold.

I remember building a fire and getting blankets, but that's all I can remember. Soon, I was asleep again.

My dreams were horrifying. I saw the Indian with one foot leading a long line of Indians carrying gold — some with cut hair, some with the scars of the whip on their backs. And Friar Nicolás was haunting me and saying, "Who is the enemy here?" I fought the blankets wrapped around me and struggled to wake up, but fell back into the nightmare again.

Friar Nicolás appeared in a fog, and the mountains glowed blood-red behind him. He held a cross of gold high over his head, its glare blinding my eyes. I woke up with the sunlight pouring through the trees.

As soon as I was able, I mounted my horse and continued on the long return journey to Taos. Although I drew the important details of the route on the map as I rode on, I never did mark any trees or arrange stones. Whenever I got off the horse, I sank to my knees. That's how weak I was from the sickness.

I carried the gold nuggets and the map in a leather bag hanging over my shoulder. I thought I would die if I let them out of my sight. I thought so many frightening things. When I began to doze again, I heard my father calling me, and tears ran down my face.

I don't know how long I went on. Maybe two days, maybe three. At night, the horse just stopped, and I slept on its back. The day came when I recognized where we were. As soon as we made it through the trees, Taos would be visible in the valley below.

Suddenly, the horse tripped on the rocks, and its front legs buckled under. I flew over its head and began to tumble over and over down the mountainside. Clutching the leather bag to my chest, I did little to protect myself as I fell and landed in a small ravine. I couldn't get up. The horse was gone.

"I'm going to die," I said aloud with great certainty. "I am surely going to die." Who would find me now?

Hours passed, giving me time to think. I looked at life in a way I never had before. Once, I had pictured life as a long adventure stretching out ahead of me. Now that it was almost over, I saw my life as a story to look back on. And what did I understand about it? I don't know.

I was a boy, born in New Mexico, who wanted to become a soldier. Was that all there was to my life? What would the story be if I lived — a boy who wanted to be a soldier and grew up to be one? No, it would be the story of a boy who found gold and grew up to be a rich soldier. But even that wasn't a story I liked. I wanted my life to mean more than that. I realized that, if I lived, I could make up the story of my life the way I wanted it to happen. I could make my life be what I wanted.

The day passed, and a night passed. Still, I couldn't get up. I slept and dreamed, and, in a waking fever, I knew my life was almost over.

Images of my family in Santa Fe, the Governor, the friars, the land and mountains, and the Indians flowed through my mind. For the first time, I saw a bigger picture of life in New Mexico. Life was about power — the Governor and the Franciscans, the soldiers and the Indians, the friars and the Indians. Even Marcos and I fought to have power over each other. As I lay there dying, it all seemed to be a terrible waste. What awful things we did to each other. Why couldn't we do something about it?

I took the gold nuggets from the leather bag at my side and laid them in a row. How different the future would be if I lived. Settlers would pour into the country from Mexico to look for gold. There would be more people, and bigger festivals. There would be new mining towns.

Mining . . . What had Friar Nicolás said about mining in New Spain? He said that thousands of Indians had died. I remembered the dream in which he had chased me. "Thousands died," he had shouted. Then I knew what I could do. I put the nuggets back into the leather bag and hugged it to my chest.

"I'm going to live," I said, and began to pray. I made a bargain with God. And I closed my eyes.

* * *

Friar Nicolás's diary:

After Marcos returned to Santa Fe, I waited at Taos eight days for Felipe to come down from the mountains. I got more worried about him as the time passed. When Felipe's horse was seen in the valley without him, the soldiers and I set out to look for him.

We had not gone very far — just up the mountainside directly east of the pueblo — when I heard Felipe crying out. He was far gone with sickness when I reached him. And, as you know, he has been here at Taos ever since.

Finishing his story has made Felipe feel better. Today he asked for food, and his sleep was more restful. The fever is broken. For the first time, I am hopeful that he will live.

* * *

Felipe's story:

I woke up with a start and looked around the adobe room. I was in a bed, and across the room sat Friar Nicolás.

"Where's my leather bag?" I asked him.

Friar Nicolás pointed to the bed and said, "There. At your side." He walked over and lifted my hand to the bag.

"I told you the story, didn't I?" I asked. "You know what's in this bag?"

"Yes."

I sat up and began to swing my legs off the bed.

Pushing me back, Friar Nicolás said, "Stay there, Felipe. You are still very sick."

I grabbed his hand. "Please help me up. There's something I must do." I stood on wobbly legs. "I'm better. Please help me."

Together we walked slowly from the room to the bright sunshine. I carried the leather bag like a baby in my arms. Pointing to an open fire in the sand, I stumbled toward it as Friar Nicolás supported me. I took the shirt on which I had drawn the map out of the leather bag. "Burn this," I said as I swayed on my feet.

Friar Nicolás helped me sit near the fire and took the shirt from me. His dark eyes looked deeply into mine.

"Burn it," I repeated. He threw the shirt into the fire, and I watched it burn with great satisfaction.

"Sit and I'll tell you the rest of my story," I said to him. "I don't know who you are, but I believe that God brought you here to be part of my life."

I rested my head on my knees for a moment before going on. "I made a bargain with God. In exchange for my life, I'm going to give Him the gold."

The friar looked surprised.

"You take the gold and have a cross made for Santa Fe. Put it in our church," I said. "You must never tell anyone where it came from. Promise me."

"I give you my word," Friar Nicolás said.

"I'll never tell anyone either. No one will ever know that I found gold in the mountains."

He asked, "Why are you doing this?"

"Maybe you won't understand this," I said. "I am deciding what the story of my life will be. I will be a soldier who gave up riches to keep New Mexico as it is, who kept a secret to stop thousands from dying."

I got up and handed him the leather bag. "I'll be a soldier who tried not to be the enemy *all* of the time."

Friar Nicolás knew what I meant. "I will bring a cross to Santa Fe," he promised.

VI

THE GOLD CROSS

Friar Nicolás's diary:
    I left New Mexico a few weeks after Felipe and I returned to Santa Fe. His family was upset that he had lied in order to go into the mountains, but was most thankful he was alive. Marcos teased him, saying that Felipe had faked the sickness as an excuse for not finding any gold.
    Felipe and I never talked about the gold again. I carried it along with me on the six-month journey back to Mexico City.
    There was still the report to do for the Viceroy. I made my decision and wrote of it to His Excellency. I told him to let New Mexico be as it is. Yes, I agreed, the times were bad. And I wrote that more trouble could be expected in the years to come. But that was no reason to abandon New Mexico.
    The Custodio and the Governor would never see eye to eye about the situation. Their struggle would continue, centering on the Indian pueblos. Such was life.
    Although the Indians were joining the Catholic faith, they would want their old ways as well. Their history was long, and the Indian dances were part of them. This struggle, too, would go on. Only time would tell how hard it would be. Christian kindness would make it easier; cruelty would make it harder. This was up to us.

I wrote about the people in Santa Fe, who were strong and determined to make a life there. I wrote about the children born since the settlers came. They were true citizens of New Mexico, who knew no other home. Do not, I wrote to the Viceroy, ask them to leave. They will make what they will of this land. And I believed they would act wisely.

I said what I did because of Felipe. The future of New Mexico could not be in better hands. The Viceroy's officials thanked me for my report, and I heard no more about it. Since the settlers are still in New Mexico, perhaps the Viceroy listened to me.

After I had been in Mexico City for a time, I located a goldsmith who could be trusted. I asked him to make a cross from the gold Felipe had given me. I did not tell him where the gold came from. In fact, I told no one.

Finally, many years later, when I had an opportunity to return to New Mexico, I brought the cross with me.

* * *

Felipe's story:

The mounted column of soldiers rode north toward Santa Fe with armor clanking as it thundered on. Marcos and I were soldiers now. We had been riding the plains, driving off the roving Indians who were attacking the pueblos.

We were returning home through a light snow in victory. None of our soldiers had been killed.

"We were splendid, don't you agree, Felipe?" Marcos shouted.

"We were," I laughed. Even though many years had passed, Marcos remained the same as the boy I grew up with.

"Not a single wound on our side," he shouted to me through the falling snow. "We drove them off in great style."

As we neared the town, the church bell rang in the thin mountain air. Through the snow, I could see that something was happening. Carts, mules, and horses filled the plaza. Many people were gathered in front of the church.

41

"Visitors," Marcos said.

Friar Nicolás was the first person I saw when I rode into the plaza. He had returned after all these years. I leaned down from my high perch on the horse to greet him.

"A fine soldier, I see," he said as he took my hand.

"As I planned to be," I said. "Welcome back to Santa Fe."

"I have the cross with me," he said, patting the leather bag he carried. "I kept my promise."

I smiled. "I knew you would."

After a Mass that served to welcome our visitors and celebrate our victory, I invited Friar Nicolás to dine at my home. I wanted him to meet my family.

"Friar Nicolás," I said later. "This is my wife, Damiana."

Damiana greeted the friar in her finest manner and said, "This is our son." She reached behind her skirts where the young boy was hiding. "His name is Felipe."

"Named for a king?" Friar Nicolás asked.

The boy stood as tall as he could and said loudly, "No, friar. I am named for my father, Captain Felipe de Ávila, who is a great soldier and leader of men."

Friar Nicolás smiled down at him. Little Felipe smiled back. My reaction had been so different when I met the friar many years ago. To me he had seemed dangerous. But my son liked him.

"Friar Nicolás saved your father's life," Damiana said, "when Father was a boy. We must all thank him for the good thing he did for us."

"Oh, then you're the friar with the dark eyes," the boy said. "I've heard the story about you. Father was sick in the mountains, and you found him. Father said he was looking for gold." He took a breath and went on. "But he never found any. Instead of gold he found life."

He looked up at me. "Isn't that how the story goes?"

"That's how the story goes, son," I said and put my hand on his head. Friar Nicolás and I exchanged a meaningful glance.

Damiana offered the friar a chair, and food was brought in. As we ate, Friar Nicolás told about his travels in Mexico, filling little

Felipe's head with visions of that great country.

The next day, Friar Nicolás stood before the church altar and spoke to the people. He held a beautiful gold cross in the air over his head so all could see it.

Damiana and little Felipe stood at my side. My mother was there with Catalina and Alonso. I wished my father were still alive to see this. Marcos stood proudly with his new bride, Maria. The world's finest woman, he always said.

"I came to Santa Fe several years ago," Friar Nicolás began. "Many of you I met then. Many of you have come here since. That visit meant a great deal to me."

He cleared his throat and continued, "Santa Fe has been in my mind and heart ever since. That is why I bring this cross to be placed in your church. It should be a sign to you to build a good country with God's blessing. The cross will remind you to care for *all* of New Mexico's people."

My son pulled at my hand, and I lifted him up.

"Are you crying, Father?" he asked, putting his little hand on my face.

"Yes."

"Because the cross is so beautiful?"

"Yes," I said.

Friar Nicolás left us for Santo Domingo a few days later. As I watched him go, I thanked God for bringing this dark-eyed stranger into my life — the stranger who helped me do something for New Mexico.

I never saw him again.

AMERICA'S PAST

The Long Journey to Santa Fe

In 1615, the only Spanish settlement in New Mexico was Santa Fe. A few Franciscan friars lived at Indian pueblos. There they built mission churches. Santa Fe lay hundreds of miles from the nearest Spanish city.

The map shows the route that Spaniards followed when they traveled to Santa Fe from Mexico City.

THE ROYAL ROAD

In the early 1600s, Mexico was part of the Spanish kingdom of New Spain. The journey from its capital of Mexico City to Santa Fe, far to the north, took six months. The way to Santa Fe was called the **Camino Real.** *That means the "Royal Road".*

The Royal Road was not a highway as you know today. There may have been rough roads to follow from Mexico City to mining towns such as Santa Barbara. But beyond these towns, the Royal Road was a simple trail over desert sands, rocks, and mountains.

On the way to Santa Fe, a long train of oxen-drawn carts slowly carried supplies along the trail. After crossing Mexico's northern desert, travelers came to the **Rio del Norte.** *This was the "River of the North," or the Rio Grande as it is known today. Here, the travelers drank and rested under cottonwood trees along the river before going on.*

The Royal Road followed the Rio del Norte until it came to a

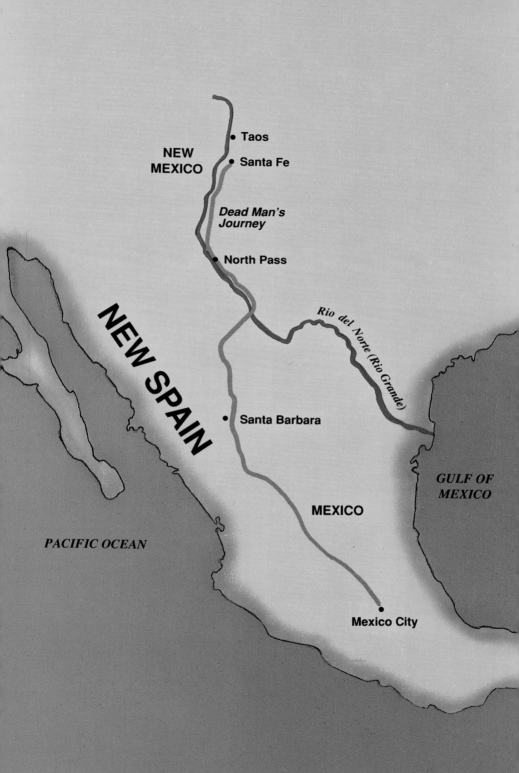

The Spanish brought wooden plows to Santa Fe in the early 1600s.

pass through the mountains. People called it the North Pass. The city of El Paso (in what is now Texas) would be built nearby years later. For sixty more miles, the Royal Road followed the river. Then the mountains along the river became steep and dangerous. The travelers had to leave the river.

The next part of the journey was through the desert. In the summer, it was too hot to travel by day. So the train of carts traveled only at night. This ninety miles of desert was called Jordada del Muerto, the "Dead Man's Journey." Finally, the travelers came to the Rio del Norte again. They began to follow the river north, passing Indian pueblos along the way.

The carts carried supplies for the settlers and missionaries in New Mexico. There were tools and materials for building. There were clothing, shoes, and bells and organs for the churches. Everyone waited eagerly for the supply train to arrive.

Oxen pulled two-wheeled wooden carts full of goods for the people in Santa Fe.

Leaving the river, the train worked its way slowly along the rocky trail that zigzagged back and forth, up the face of a steep cliff. At the top was the great plain of Santa Fe with high mountains to the east. From here, people could see the settlement of Santa Fe across the plain. That's where the Royal Road ended. The six-month journey was over.